This book belongs to :

Georgie and the Computer Bugs

Georgie and the Computer Bugs

Text © 1995 Julia Jarman

Illustrations © 1995 Damon Burnard

ISBN 0713640154

First published in 1995

by A & C Black (Publishers) Ltd., England

喬琪與電腦蟲

Julia Jarman 著

Damon Burnard 繪

刊欣媒體營造工作室 譯

三民書局

Chapter One

Georgie Bell was off computers — right off. **Weird** things had been happening recently. She'd been sucked in twice! Yes, really! Into her computer! And she'd nearly been eaten by a dragon. Her **brilliant** brain had **saved** her — just — but she was **definitely** going to get a new hobby.

第一章

　　喬琪貝兒剛剛關上電腦。最近發生了一些怪事，喬琪已經被吸進電腦兩次了！真的，她真的被自己的電腦吸進去，還差點被一條龍吃掉！還好，她的聰明才智救了她，不過，喬琪已經打算培養電腦之外的另一種興趣了。

　　沒錯！找個安全一點的興趣……

　　譬如說……高空彈跳！

weird [wɪrd] 形 不可思議的

brilliant [`brɪljənt] 形 頭腦機敏的

save [sev] 動 救

definitely [`dɛfənɪtlɪ] 副 明確地

She put a cloth over the computer.

What now?

It was while she was **looking for** something to do that she heard a voice.

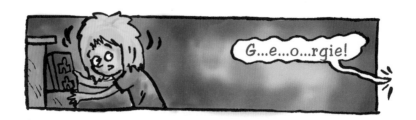

At first she thought it was the Tank, her **pestiferous** little sister, but even the Tank — who could have **spied** for MI5 — couldn't get under that cloth. And that's where the voice was coming from.

她拿了一塊布蓋在電腦上。

呵！眼不見為淨！

接下來，該做什麼呢？

正當她左思右想的時候，突然聽到了一個聲音。

喬⋯⋯喬⋯⋯喬琪⋯⋯

剛開始，她以為是煩人的小妹唐可，不過，就算是唐可——一心想去英國情報處保安部當間諜——也沒辦法躲在那塊布底下。聲音就是從那兒傳出來的。

look for 尋找

pestiferous [pɛsˋtɪfərəs] 形 煩人的

spy [spaɪ] 動 當間諜

It was a **hoarse** voice. **Carefully** Georgie lifted the edge of the cloth.

Oh no! A dragon voice.

She dropped the cloth.

It was a hoarse dragon voice to be **precise**, and Georgie knew exactly which dragon it was.

喬⋯⋯喬⋯⋯喬琪⋯⋯

聲音聽起來很粗啞，喬琪小心翼翼地掀起布的一角。

喬⋯⋯喬⋯⋯喬琪⋯⋯

天哪！是龍的叫聲！

她立刻把布蓋上。

真的是龍的叫聲，而且，喬琪認得那條龍。

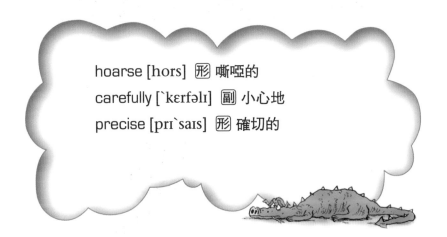

hoarse [hors] 形 嘶啞的

carefully [`kɛrfəlɪ] 副 小心地

precise [prɪ`saɪs] 形 確切的

Georgie **covered** her ears and walked away. This was even weirder than before. The computer wasn't even **plugged in**!

就是那條龍想吃掉我……

……兩次！

喬琪！喬琪！妳一定要救救我！

不！門兒都沒有！

　喬琪搗著耳朵走開，這一次，比以前更詭異，因為電腦根本沒插電！

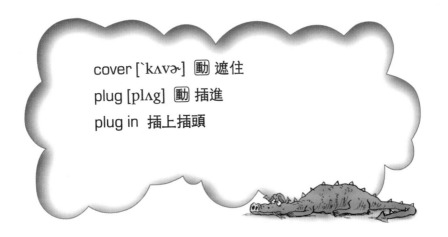

cover [`kʌvɚ] 動 遮住

plug [plʌg] 動 插進

plug in 插上插頭

Chapter Two

*G*eorgie **paced** the room.

But it was too late. The Tank was already in.

Definitely too late — she was **lifting** the cloth.

第二章

喬琪在房間裡走來走去。

我什麼都不知道，跟我一點兒關係都沒有！

叩！叩！叩！

喬琪，妳在跟誰說話啊？

沒有哇！唐可，不要進來！

來不及了，唐可已經走進來了。

真的來不及了！因為她把布掀開來了！

喬琪！喬琪！

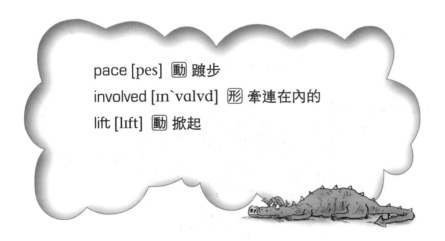

pace [pes] 動 踱步
involved [ɪn`valvd] 形 牽連在內的
lift [lɪft] 動 掀起

The dragon was still **begging** for help and his voice was weaker now.

Georgie looked.

The dragon looked terrible. His nose was running and his fire had **gone out**. His face was covered with spots — purple spots with yellow centers that *glowed* — and he was shaking **violently**.

那條龍還在苦苦哀求，而且聲音聽起來更虛弱了。

好可憐喔！沒關係，我們來幫你。喬琪，你看！

喬琪看著他。

那條龍看起來真的很糟，不但火焰熄了，還流著鼻涕，而且臉上長滿紫色的疹子，疹子中央還黃得發亮呢！而且，他不停地發抖。

好……好冷！喬琪，我真……真的……好冷！

就算妳不幫我，也請救救我的孩子吧！他們沒傷害過妳啊！

beg [bɛg] 動 請求；乞求 《for》

go out 熄滅

glow [glo] 動 燃燒般發光

violently [ˋvaɪələntlɪ] 副 劇烈地

He moved aside to let Georgie see his children, **huddled** in a four-poster bed.

'Where are you?' said Georgie.

'I don't know,' said the dragon. 'I've taken a room in some **ancient hostelry**. We were on our way home when the bugs **struck**.'

Only then did Georgie notice the disc in the disc drive.

他閃到一旁，好讓喬琪看看他縮在床上的孩子們。

妳看！

「你們在哪兒呢？」喬琪問。

「我也不知道，」那條龍回答，「我們正在回家的路上，卻遇上電腦蟲的攻擊，現在只好住在一家古老的客棧裡。」

這時候，喬琪注意到磁碟機裡的磁片。

龍族回鄉記

huddle [ˋhʌdl̩] 動 擠成一團
ancient [ˋenʃənt] 形 古老的
hostelry [ˋhɑstl̩rɪ] 名 客棧
strike [straɪk] 動 突然侵襲

'Poor Daphne. Poor Dennis. Poor Deidre,' said the Tank. All three were covered with spots that glowed, and their teeth were **chattering**.

The dragon did look ill, but Georgie still didn't **trust** him. It might be a **trick**.

「可憐的黛芬，可憐的丹尼，可憐的荻莉。」唐可說。他們的牙齒不停地打顫，臉上都是發熱的疹子。

水……我要喝……水……

我已經幫不了他們了，喬琪，我們需要妳！

雖然那條龍看起來已經奄奄一息，不過，喬琪還是有點懷疑，說不定那只是個詭計。

chatter [ˋtʃætɚ] 動 咯咯作響

trust [trʌst] 動 信任

trick [trɪk] 名 欺詐；騙局

The dragon waved weakly at the window. 'Look at all those graves,' he said.

'Because it's a *computer* virus, G...e...orgie, and you're the computer **ace** — aren't you? There are bugs in the system.' This last speech **exhausted** him and he **collapsed** beside the bed.

那條龍蹣跚地走向窗邊說：「看看那些墳墓！」

我們都感染了致命的病毒，喬琪，如果妳不救我們，我們就活不了多久了！

為什麼選上我呢？

「因為那是電腦病毒啊！喬……喬琪，妳是個電腦高手吧？電腦系統裡面有蟲啊！」這一番話耗盡了龍的所有力氣，一說完，他就癱在床邊了。

哎！

virus [ˈvaɪrəs] 名 病毒

ace [es] 名 高手

exhaust [ɪgˈzɔst] 動 耗盡

collapse [kəˈlæps] 動 不支倒下

Chapter Three

$\mathcal{G}$eorgie
thought
about it.

Bugs in the system were quite **common** and sometimes the cure was easy. You just **switched off** and they **disappeared**. She'd try that — and switch off the dragon at the same time!

Warily — she didn't want to get too close — she reached out and switched OFF, with the tip of her finger.

Nothing happened! The dragon was still there and so were his children.

第三章

喬琪想了一下。

嗯……

電腦蟲不是什麼大不了的問題，通常也很好解決，關機以後，他們就會不見了。於是，她試了這個方法——順便讓那些龍都同時消失掉！

她小心翼翼地，甚至不敢靠太近，終於用指尖按下了關機鍵。

啪！

什麼事都沒發生，大龍和小龍還在！

common [`kɑmən] 形 司空見慣的

switch off 關掉開關

disappear [ˌdɪsə`pɪr] 動 消失

warily [`wɛrəlɪ] 副 小心翼翼地

She **peered** behind the computer. It still wasn't plugged in, so what was going on? And where were those bugs?

Georgie still **suspected foul play**, but she could see something in the corner of the screen.

真是太詭異了！

救救我們啊！

她看看電腦後面，還是沒插電啊！到底是怎麼回事呢？那些電腦蟲又在哪兒呢？

唐可，妳看得到蟲嗎？

有啊！

在那裡⋯⋯還有那裡⋯⋯

喬琪還是不太相信，不過，她真的看到螢幕一角有個東西。

糟了！

⋯⋯還有那裡！

peer [pɪr] 勔 盯著看

suspect [sə`spɛkt] 勔 懷疑

foul play 卑鄙的行為

It was an evil-looking **creature** with four eyes. Sparks **zig-zagged** off its wiry **feelers**.

It's...it's like the butcher's electric fly-catcher!

She was right. Something went too close...

那是一隻醜陋的四眼怪物，扭曲的觸角還不時冒出火花。

看⋯⋯看起來好像屠夫的電動捕蠅器！

她說的沒錯。接著，有個東西太靠近他了⋯⋯

嗡⋯⋯嗡⋯⋯

creature [`kritʃɚ] 名 生物

zig-zag [`zɪgzæg] 動 呈Z字形前進

feeler [`filɚ] 名 觸角

...and it was gone.

Electric! Of course! Georgie's brain worked fast. The bugs were electric, **generating** their own **electricity**.

So that's why the computer didn't need to be plugged in!

There are lots of bugs, Georgie!

The Tank was **pointing** at them. Georgie pulled her away.

Careful, Tank! Get back!

嘶嘶……

唉唷！

咕嚕！

……然後就不見了。

電力！沒錯，喬琪的腦筋飛快地思考著。這些蟲都是電動的，自己就能發電。

所以，即使電腦沒插電，他們也能活動。

好多蟲喔！喬琪！

唐可指著那些蟲，喬琪立刻拉開她。

小心！唐可，退後一點！

electric [ɪˋlɛktrɪk] 形 電的
generate [ˋdʒɛnə‚ret] 動 產生
electricity [ɪ‚lɛkˋtrɪsətɪ] 名 電力
point [pɔɪnt] 動 指 《at》

There was a row of dirty white ones on the edge of the pillow behind the young dragons' heads.

There were clusters of yellow ones on the bed curtains. Every now and again one of them **flashed**.

'See,' the dragon's voice was faint.

Georgie did see — and it made her even more **determined** to **stay out of** it.

小龍躺著的枕頭旁是一整排髒兮兮的白色小蟲。

床單上也滿是黃色的小蟲，還不時發出閃光。

「看到了吧！」大龍的聲音更加虛弱了。

這裡已經被他們佔領了！

他們已經取得優勢了！

喬琪看得一清二楚，也更加深了她置身事外的決心。

flash [flæʃ] 動 閃爍

take over 接管

determine [dɪ`tɝmɪn] 動 決心

stay out of... 避開……

Chapter Four

*T*he Tank was determined to stay.

Fortunately, Georgie **managed** to **drag** Tank on to the landing.

Unfortunately, she **tripped** over the cat, and Tank shot back into the room.

第四章

唐可，我們離開這裡！

不行！等一下！

唐可決定留下來。

快來啊！

我會幫助你們的！

求求妳們，別走哇！

幸運的是，喬琪終於把唐可拖出了房間。

但不幸的是，喬琪被貓絆倒，唐可就趁機跑回房間去了。

喔——謝謝你了，臭貓！

fortunately [`fɔrtʃənɪtlɪ] 副 幸運地

manage [`mænɪdʒ] 動 設法

drag [dræg] 動 拖；拉

trip [trɪp] 動 絆倒 《over》

Georgie shot after her.

But Tank's finger was already on the
ENTER key and...

...the computer was **roaring** like a hungry
hoover.

喬琪追著妹妹。

唐可，不可以！

大龍小龍，我來了！

可是，唐可已經摸到了「確認(ENTER)」鍵，然後……

不要！

……電腦變成了一部強力吸塵器。

roar [ror] 動 吼叫

hoover [`huvɚ] 名 真空吸塵器

Georgie **dived** for the Tank's legs but...

...it was too late.

Georgie **pounded** the RETURN key. She pounded the EXIT key. She held it down. She prayed. And the spinning screen went into **reverse**.

喬琪衝上前去，想拉住唐可的腳，但是……

唐可，回來啊！

……太遲了！

喬琪敲打著「退回(RETURN)」鍵，又敲擊著「跳出(EXIT)」鍵。她把按鍵按住不放，不停地祈禱著，旋轉中的電腦畫面開始逆轉。

唐可？

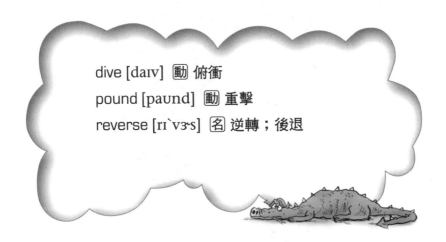

dive [daɪv] 勔 俯衝

pound [paʊnd] 勔 重擊

reverse [rɪ`vɝs] 名 逆轉；後退

There was a flash like lightning, and out of the screen crawled...

A BUG!

Georgie **squished** it...

...but another appeared...

...and another!

突然間，一道亮光閃過，螢幕上出現了……

一隻蟲！

喬琪立刻殲滅他……

砰！

……又出現一隻……

……還有一隻！

squish [skwɪʃ] 動 壓扁

Then the face of an **enormous** bug filled
the screen.

Its voice sizzled with **satisfaction**.

'Sssss...uper Bug at your service, Ma'am.'
The creature bowed,
and a red
something on
the top of its
head wobbled.

接下來，螢幕上出現了蟲老大。

喬琪，妳想消滅我們，可沒那麼簡單！

我們有千千萬萬隻！

他的嘶嘶聲中充滿了驕傲。

「嘶……嘶……，女士，蟲老大隨時候教！」他做個鞠躬的動作，頭頂上紅色的東西還不斷搖晃著。

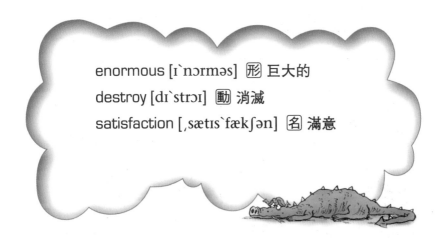

enormous [ɪ`nɔrməs] 形 巨大的

destroy [dɪ`strɔɪ] 動 消滅

satisfaction [ˌsætɪs`fækʃən] 名 滿意

'We're taking over, you ss...ee.'

It sizzled again. 'We've sss...tarted, and s...so we'll finish. Ha!'

Suddenly Georgie **remembered** Tank. Where was she?

Any moment now her mother would be calling them for dinner.

「我們就要贏了，妳瞧！」

他又發出嘶嘶的聲音，「一切由我們……嘶……嘶……開始，也由我們結……束。哈！」

喬琪忽然想起唐可，她在哪兒？

媽媽隨時會來叫她們吃晚飯的。

我必須採取行動，我得把唐可救回來！

妳辦不到的，哈！哈！哈！

噫！他好像能夠讀出我的心思！

沒錯，喬琪！這兒有個思想偵測器。

remember [rɪ`mɛmbɚ] 動 想起

detector [dɪ`tɛktɚ] 名 探測器

'We're so **powerful**, Georgie. We've **wiped out** whole programs. We've **ruined** banks.'

It was true. Georgie had read about it in the papers.

But — Georgie cheered up — she'd read about something else too.

She remembered an **advertisement** in *Computer Weekly*:

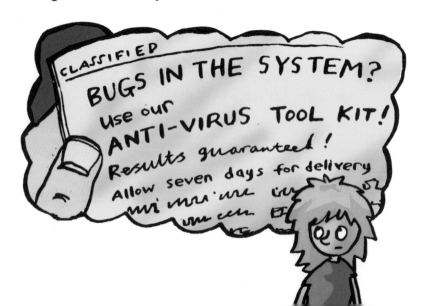

「我們很強大，喬琪，整個電腦程式都被我們破壞了，連銀行也完蛋了！」

我們把政府搞垮了！

這是真的，喬琪在報上看過這個消息。

不過——喬琪露出微笑——她還從報上看到了其他的報導。

她記得《電腦週報》上的一則廣告：

分類廣告

電腦系統內有蟲嗎？

請用我們的防毒工具組！

保證有效！

運送期七天……

powerful [ˋpaʊəfəl] 形 強大的

wipe out 清除

ruin [ˋruɪn] 動 毀滅

bring down 打敗

advertisement [͵ædvəˋtaɪzmənt] 名 廣告

She had to think of a plan, fast.

More bugs were **tumbling** out of the disc drive...

...dropping on to the **keyboard**...

...and rolling on to the floor.

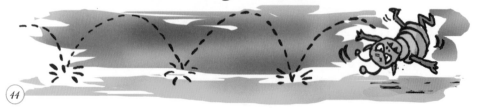

聽起來不錯……

……可是我等不了七天！

她必須另外想辦法，而且要快！

越來越多的電腦蟲從磁碟機裡跑出來……

……掉到鍵盤上……

……又滾到地板上。

tumble [`tʌmbl̩] 動 滾下

keyboard [`ki,bord] 名 鍵盤

Chapter Five

Georgie ran to the bathroom.

It would have to be DIY.

In seconds she was back with the bottle.
Bugs were **germs**, weren't they?

Georgie **squirted furiously** at the bugs
near her feet.

第五章

喬琪跑到浴室裡。

必須靠自己了！

呵！這個一定有用。

殺蟲劑

幾秒鐘後，她帶著那瓶殺蟲劑回到房間。電腦蟲也是一種小蟲嘛！

喬琪拿著殺蟲劑朝腳邊的電腦蟲拼命噴灑。

來吧！

來吧！

咻！咻！

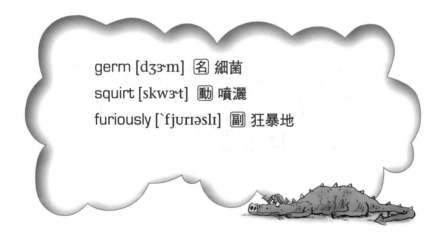

germ [dʒɝm] 名 細菌

squirt [skwɝt] 動 噴灑

furiously [`fjʊrɪəslɪ] 副 狂暴地

'It won't work, Georgie,' Super Bug was *laughing*.

The bugs **vanished** beneath the spray, but they soon reappeared.

Georgie squirted again.

But the bugs fought back, and as the bottle ran dry they **emerged** from the foam, shaking themselves like small wet dogs.

'HA! HA! HA! HA! HA! HA!' Super Bug was having **convulsions** of laughter.

「沒用的，喬琪。」蟲老大笑著。

沒用的！

不會成功的！

電腦蟲雖然在受殺蟲劑攻擊時會暫時消失，但卻很快又出現了。

喬琪只好再次噴灑。

可是電腦蟲開始反擊，當整瓶殺蟲劑都噴完時，蟲子們從殺蟲劑的泡沫中探出頭來，像一隻濕淋淋的小狗一樣搖擺著身體，甩掉泡沫。

「哈！哈！哈！哈！哈！哈！」蟲老大狂笑著。

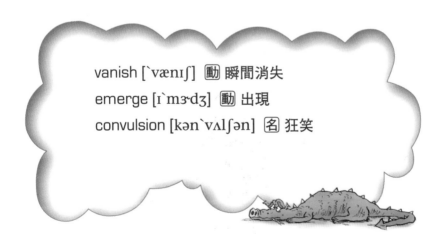

vanish [`vænɪʃ] 動 瞬間消失

emerge [ɪ`mɝdʒ] 動 出現

convulsion [kən`vʌlʃən] 名 狂笑

Super Bug was **exultant**. 'That **label** says "Kills all KNOWN germs", Georgie, but...' he was laughing so much he could hardly talk.

Georgie **raised** her foot, but as she brought it down...

妳是在浪費時間，喬琪！

妳不認識字嗎？

蟲老大非常得意，「瓶子上的標籤明明寫著『對付所有已知的蟲子』，喬琪，而……」他笑到連話都說不下去了。

我們是不知名的蟲子啊！不是嗎？

喬琪抬起腳來，而當她把腳放下時……

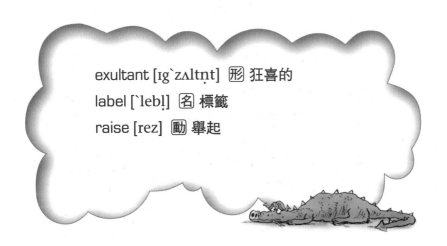

exultant [ɪgˋzʌltn̩t] 形 狂喜的
label [ˋlebl̩] 名 標籤
raise [rez] 動 舉起

...the bugs rose in a **swarm**, then **hung** from the lampshade.

……蟲子們聚集成群，從燈罩上懸垂下來。

swarm [swɔrm] 名 一群
hang [hæŋ] 動 吊掛

Time was running out.

She studied the keyboard.

DELETE? She might delete Tank.

SEARCH? That was better. She must find the Tank.

Above her the bugs hummed.

Georgie didn't like leaving them **on the loose,** but she hadn't much **choice.**

沒時間了。

我得想想別的法子。

她研究著電腦鍵盤。

「刪除(DELETE)」？可能會把唐可一起刪除掉。

「搜尋(SEARCH)」？應該比較適當，她必須找到唐可。

電腦蟲在喬琪的頭頂上不停地嗡嗡叫著。

嘿！嘿！嘿！

妳沒辦法把我們打死做太妃糖的！

喬琪不喜歡那些蟲得意的樣子，不過也拿他們沒辦法。

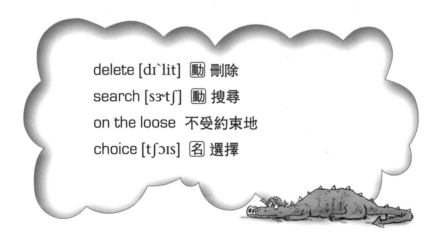

delete [dɪ`lit] 動 刪除

search [sɝtʃ] 動 搜尋

on the loose 不受約束地

choice [tʃɔɪs] 名 選擇

She pressed SEARCH, and a mountainous **terrain** appeared.

She pressed again. This time she got the dragon's **lair**.

The door was open but there was no **sign** of the dragons. No sign of the Tank either.

She pressed SEARCH again.

她按下「搜尋(SEARCH)」鍵，接著螢幕上出現一處山區的景象。

唔……沒有唐可的蹤跡！

再按一次，這次喬琪找到龍的巢穴。

龍的巢穴

請勿靠近

門是開著的，但沒有龍的蹤跡，也沒有唐可的蹤跡。

喬琪再按一次「搜尋(SEARCH)」鍵。

terrain [tɛ`ren] 名 地形

lair [lɛr] 名 （野獸的）窩；巢；穴

sign [saɪn] 名 跡象

This looked more **promising**.

A village appeared. It seemed to be **deserted**, but she thought she **recognized** the ancient hostelry.

Were the dragons in there?

Was the Tank?

Georgie knew she'd have to go in.

A cabbagey smell was climbing the stairs.

Her mother would be close behind.

這次看起來比較有希望了。

螢幕上出現一個村莊，這個村莊看起來似乎已經荒廢了，不過喬琪認出了那是一家古老的客棧。

龍會在裡面嗎？

唐可也在那兒嗎？

喬琪知道自己必須進去一趟。

一陣飯菜的香味飄上樓來。

食物的味道

喔，糟了！

媽媽就快來了。

promising [ˋprɑmɪsɪŋ] 形 有希望的
deserted [dɪˋzɝtɪd] 形 荒廢的
recognize [ˋrɛkəɡˏnaɪz] 動 認得

Chapter Six

Quickly she **flicked** through the **menus**.

第六章

我應該帶什麼東西呢？

她很快地檢閱過清單。

武器

　1.弓

　2.劍

　3.戟

唔……

好像沒有一樣用得上！

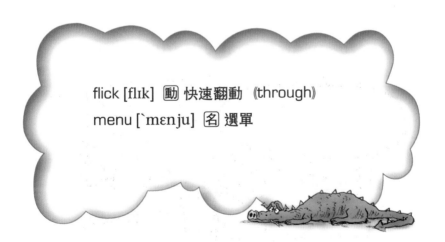

flick [flɪk] 動 快速翻動 《through》

menu [ˋmɛnju] 名 選單

Another menu came up.

An idea was beginning to come to her. She really needed more time to think, but her mother was in an **impatient** mood.

接著出現另一頁清單。

工具

 1.馬

 2.手電筒

 3.無底袋

我想應該帶手電筒！

還有什麼呢？

喬琪想到了一個主意。她實在需要更多時間來思考，不過她媽媽已經不耐煩了。

晚飯好了，叫唐可一起下來吧，聽到了沒？

impatient [ɪmˋpeʃənt] 形 不耐煩的

'No ifs, Georgie! If you're not down it ten seconds flat there'll be trouble!' she yelled.

Georgie plugged in her computer.

She **reckoned** that if she did **defeat** the bugs — and she had to — she would need an electricity supply to **get out** again.

如果可以的話，媽！

「沒有如果，喬琪！如果妳們不在十秒鐘之內下樓來，妳們就糟糕了！」她叫著。

10……9……8……7……

喬琪把電腦的電源插上。

她想，如果她真的打敗電腦蟲──她必須打敗他們──她會需要電力從電腦裡出來。

……6……5……4……

reckon [ˋrɛkən] 動 認為

defeat [dɪˋfit] 動 打敗

get out 出來

Then Georgie pressed ENTER.

But by the time Mrs Bell entered
Georgie's bedroom...

...Georgie had gone.

然後喬琪按下「確認(ENTER)」鍵。

我來了，唐可！

3……2……1……，我要進來了！

就在貝兒太太進到喬琪房間之前……

……喬琪已經不見了。

Chapter Seven

VROOSH!

$\mathcal{T}$hrough the computer screen and aeons of time into...

...a medieval village where Super Bug and his troops were waiting.

第七章

VROOSH!

咻！

穿過電腦螢幕和時光隧道來到……

……一個中世紀的村莊，蟲老大和他的電腦蟲軍隊正在那兒等著。

Battle was about to begin.

Score so far:

Georgie
17
(the squished and squashed bugs)

Bugs
1,999,993
(their **victims**)

Fortunately, the bugs didn't see Georgie arrive because Mrs Bell had plunged the scene into darkness while trying to **turn off** the computer.

戰爭就要開始。

到目前為止，雙方得分為：

喬琪　17（被踩扁和打扁的電腦蟲數目）

電腦蟲　1,999,993（受害者數目）

　　幸運的是，電腦蟲沒有發現喬琪的到來，因為貝兒太太要關電腦的時候，把螢幕調暗了。

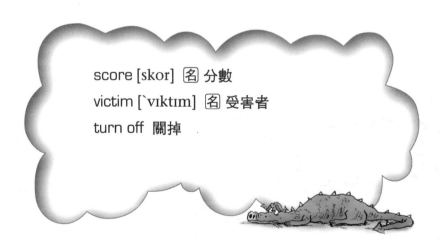

score [skor] 名 分數

victim [ˋvɪktɪm] 名 受害者

turn off 關掉

Unfortunately, Georgie couldn't see much either — only from time to time a tiny flashing light — but the torch was useful.

The bugs made a noise like the hum of a fridge. Georgie looked all around.

不幸的是，喬琪也看不清楚了──只有偶爾出現的
微弱閃光──不過手電筒就派上用場了。

我知道你們在這兒……

我看得見也聽得見你們！

嗡！

嘶嘶！

電腦蟲發出像冰箱一樣的嗡嗡聲。喬琪四處張望著。

嗯……

On three sides were cottages and on the other a church. Here and there a spotty body **slumped** against a wall.

She could just **make out** a notice saying BRING OUT YOUR DEAD. It was **leaning** against a cart piled high with bodies — all of them covered with the dreaded purple and yellow spots.

有三面都是小村舍，另一面則是一座教堂。到處都有身上滿是斑點的人癱坐在牆角。

噫！

她好不容易才辨認出一塊寫著「屍體放置處」的指示牌，牌子就靠在一輛堆滿屍體的小貨車上——所有的屍體上都佈滿著紫色及黃色的可怕斑點。

屍體放置處

slump [slʌmp] 動 癱坐

make out 好不容易才看出

lean [lin] 動 靠 《against》

In the graveyard was a sign saying FULL.

There were crosses on many of the cottage doors and on the door of *Ye Travellers (Last) Rest*.

墳場上，有一塊牌子寫著「客滿」。

墓地客滿

許多小村舍的門上都有十字架，「旅客（最後）休息處」的門上也有。

也許這就是大龍所提到的古老客棧。

旅客休息處

There was a **dim** light in an upstairs
window. Georgie decided she must go in.

Two voices answered her from different
directions.

said one voice.

said the other.

Georgie followed the first voice and found
herself in a cowshed facing a cow's bottom.

樓上的窗口有一盞微弱的燈光，喬琪決定進去看看。

唐可也許會在那兒！

哈囉？有人在嗎？

從不同的方向傳來兩聲回答。

我在後面。

第一個聲音說。

我在樓上。

另一個聲音說。

喬琪沿著第一個聲音的方向走去，進到一處牛棚，看見一頭牛的屁股。

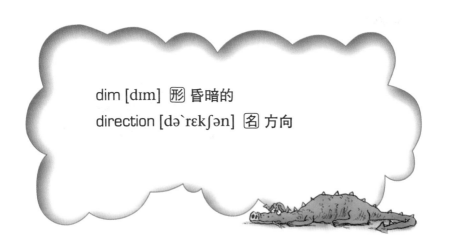

dim [dɪm] 形 昏暗的
direction [dəˋrɛkʃən] 名 方向

said the cow.

screamed a milkmaid.

And Georgie had a BRILLIANT thought.

哞！

那頭牛叫著。

啊！

擠牛奶的婦人尖叫出聲。

然後，喬琪想到一個很好的辦法。

What had happened was this:

1. The milkmaid saw Georgie and screamed.

She had never seen a twentieth century person before and thought Georgie was a ghost or evil spirit.

2. The cow, hearing the milkmaid scream, **kicked** the bucket — which hit Georgie's leg, at the same time as milk from its **udders** squirted into her eye.

事情發生的經過是這樣的：

1.擠牛奶的婦人看見喬琪後尖叫。

噫！

這是魔法嗎！

因為她從沒見過二十世紀的人，所以她以為喬琪是鬼魂或惡魔。

2.那頭牛聽到婦人的尖叫後，踢翻了牛奶桶，桶子又撞到喬琪的腳，同時，乳牛身上噴出的乳汁濺到喬琪的眼睛。

哎！

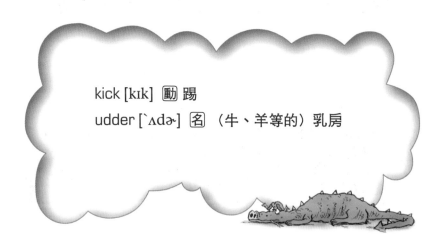

kick [kɪk] 動 踢

udder [`ʌdɚ] 名 （牛、羊等的）乳房

3. Georgie turned to look at the milkmaid and was **amazed** by what she saw.

And the cow MOO-ed.

3.喬琪轉過身看著婦人，對於自己所看到的情況感到非常驚訝。

什麼？沒有斑點？為什麼？其他人身上都有啊！

接著牛「哞」地叫了一聲。

哞！

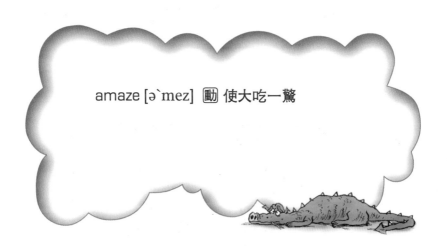

amaze [əˋmez] 動 使大吃一驚

And this led to Georgie's great **discovery**. Call it déjà vu, or déjà moo or even déjà poo (for the cow's breath was **disgusting**), whatever, Georgie had the answer — *im-moo-nisation*!

At that moment she heard the Tank's voice from upstairs.

Georgie knew what she had to do.

這使得喬琪有了大發現。你可以叫牠做「阿哞」、「哞哞」或「嗚哞」（因為牛吐出來的氣息很難聞），無論如何，喬琪得到解答了——就是「哞」的聲音！

　　婦人身上沒有斑點，是因為她和牛在一起工作！

　　她一定常常聽到「哞」的聲音！

　　就在那個時候，喬琪聽到唐可的聲音從樓上傳來。

　　喬琪，救命啊！

　　喬琪知道她該怎麼做了。

　　嗯……我能不能借用一下妳的牛……只要牠叫一聲就好了？

discovery [dɪ`skʌvrɪ]　名 發現

disgusting [dɪs`gʌstɪŋ]　形 令人作嘔的

Chapter Eight

It was hard getting the cow upstairs, but as she pulled and sometimes pushed, Georgie had an **inspiring** thought. She would take her place among those famous men and women who had pushed back the **frontiers** of science and saved the world from life-**threatening** diseases.

第八章

　　要把那頭牛弄到樓上實在很困難，當她又拉又推地努力時，喬琪又有了一個令人興奮的想法。她將自己想像成那些推動科學及拯救人類生命的名人。

　　嘿咻！居禮夫人！亞歷山大佛萊明！現在……呼……呼……喬琪貝兒！

inspiring [ɪn`spaɪrɪŋ] 形 鼓舞人心的
frontier [frʌn`tɪr] 名 （知識的）最先進的領域
threatening [`θrɛtn̩ɪŋ] 形 威脅的

At last Georgie and the cow reached the top.

And there was the Tank, looking every bit a Florence Nightingale, **tending** the dragons, though she herself didn't look well.

Georgie **signaled** to her to keep quiet, but it was too late. The bugs had heard everything. And they hadn't been **idle**.

最後，喬琪和那頭牛終於到達樓上。

呼！

哞！

唐可就在那兒，看起來好像南丁格爾，正在照顧著大龍和小龍，儘管她自己看起來也不怎麼好。

喬琪向唐可做手勢要她別出聲，不過，太遲了。電腦蟲已經聽見一切，他們可沒閒著。

tend [tɛnd] 動 照顧

signal [`sɪgn̩] 動 發信號 《to》

idle [`aɪd̩l] 形 無所事事的

Already the score was:

Georgie	Bugs
17	1,999,994

Their latest victim was the village bell-ringer. He'd been hanging on, but the battle for life had finally become too much for him.

As he **let go of** the rope, the bell **tolled** and Super Bug gave the signal to attack...

...and the bugs **descended**.

雙方的分數為：

喬琪　17

電腦蟲　1,999,994

新受害者是村裡的敲鐘手。他一直都很盡忠職守，但他終究沒能在這場生死戰役中存活下來。

再見，殘酷的世界！

當他放開繩子時，鐘聲響起，蟲老大也下達攻擊的信號⋯⋯

向前衝⋯⋯

獲得勝利！

⋯⋯然後電腦蟲便展開攻擊。

let go of... 放開⋯⋯

toll [tol] 動 敲響

descend [dɪ`sɛnd] 動 突然襲擊

Fortunately, the cow, who couldn't **stand** the sound of bells, moo-ed **mournfully**.

MOO and bugs met **head-on**.

The moo was quite powerful.

A few bugs fell to the ground.

幸運的是，那頭牛無法忍受鐘聲，發出痛苦的「哞」聲。

牛的「哞」聲和電腦蟲正面衝突。

「哞！」

這一聲「哞」非常有力。

有一些電腦蟲跌落地面。

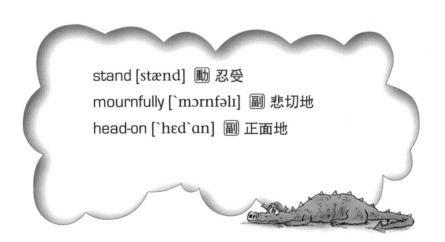

stand [stænd] 動 忍受
mournfully [`mɔrnfəlɪ] 副 悲切地
head-on [`hɛd`ɑn] 副 正面地

After the first round the score was:

Georgie 169	Bugs 1,999,994

Super Bug **ordered** the bugs to re-**group**.

They did — into two swarms.

第一回合之後，雙方得分為：

喬琪　169

電腦蟲　1,999,994

蟲老大命令電腦蟲們再次集結。

蟲子們集合了——分成兩隊。

攻擊！

order [ˋɔrdɚ] 動 命令

group [grup] 動 集合

After Round Two the score was:

Georgie & Cow	Bugs
589	1,999,994

Super Bug grew angry.

YOU CALL THAT AN ATTACK?

YOU SHOULD BE ASHAMED OF YOURSELVES!

He ordered the bugs to attack **properly**, and this time they did.

Unfortunately, the cow was eating some leaves growing through the window. Georgie couldn't **persuade** her to leave them.

CHOMP!
CHEW!

Come on, Cow! We need you!

第二回合之後，分數變成：

喬琪和牛　589

電腦蟲　1,999,994

蟲老大生氣了。

你們這叫攻擊嗎？

你們不會感到丟臉嗎？

他命令蟲子們徹底攻擊，這次他們做對了。

　不幸的是，牛正在吃著窗外的葉子，而喬琪無法使牠離開那些葉子。

　來吧，牛！我們需要你！

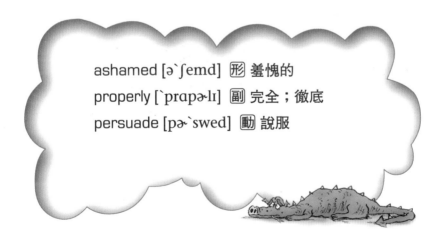

ashamed [əˋʃemd] 形 羞愧的

properly [ˋprɑpɚlɪ] 副 完全；徹底

persuade [pɚˋswed] 動 說服

For several minutes the bugs did their worst. They stung, sizzled and bit.

The Tank **swatted**, **splatted** and **stamped**, and actually managed to squish a few.

Georgie **urged** the cow to moo but it went on chomping the leaves.

來吧！

攻擊！

抓住他們！

電腦蟲進行了數分鐘的猛烈攻擊，他們嘶嘶地叫著，對敵人又叮又咬。

試試這個！

咯吱！

唐可用力拍擊、踩踏，確實踩扁了一些電腦蟲。

喬琪努力要讓牛發出「哞」的叫聲，但是那頭牛卻還是不停地吃著樹葉。

swat [swɑt] 動 重拍

splat [splæt] 動 碰撞後變平

stamp [stæmp] 動 踩

urge [ɝdʒ] 動 催趕

From his **vantage point** on the headboard, Super Bug crackled **hysterically**. 'Ha ha HA! Any second now, Georgie Bell, you'll be covered with spots!'

You'll feel terrible in a minute!

But no spots appeared on Georgie.

She didn't feel terrible. She felt quite well. So did the Tank!

Immoonisation was working!

The score was now:

We're catching up!

Bah!

Georgie & Cow & Tank	Bugs
1012	1,999,994

蟲老大站在床頭觀望，歇斯底里地叫著，「哈！哈！哈！從現在起，喬琪貝兒，妳的身上將會長滿斑點！」

一分鐘之內，妳們就會完蛋了！

但是喬琪身上沒有出現斑點。

她沒有覺得不舒服，她覺得很好，唐可也是一樣！

牛的「哞」聲發生作用了！

雙方得分為：

我們就要趕上你們了！

可惡！

喬琪、牛和唐可　1012

電腦蟲　1,999,994

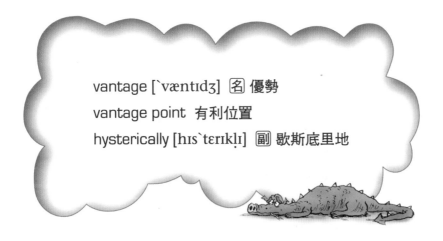

vantage [`væntɪdʒ] 名 優勢

vantage point 有利位置

hysterically [hɪs`tɛrɪklɪ] 副 歇斯底里地

Super Bug grew **furious**.

Georgie **explained** to the Tank about immoonisation. 'If the cow doesn't moo we can't fight back,' said Georgie, 'and she's clearly not in the mood.'

蟲老大非常憤怒。

哼！

喀滋！

快點！我們必須幫助大龍和小龍！

我不知道耶，唐可，我們應該回家……

我會逮到妳們的！

喬琪向唐可解釋「哞」聲的效果，「如果那頭牛不發出『哞』的叫聲，我們就無法反擊，但是牠顯然沒有心情。」

我們試試看這樣……

furious [`fjʊrɪəs] 形 暴怒的

explain [ɪk`splen] 動 解釋

The Tank pulled the cow's tail — and the cow was not pleased. Her moos filled the room. The noise was terrible.

The smell was worse, but the effect was miraculous. As Georgie and the Tank watched, the dragons' spots started to fade.

哞！

唐可，妳看！

　　唐可拉扯牛的尾巴，使得牛很不高興，「哞」的叫聲充滿了整個房間，聽起來很可怕。

　　隨著牛的叫聲所呼出的氣味很難聞，不過這一叫卻
有不可思議的效果。在喬琪和唐可的注視下，大龍小龍
身上的斑點開始消褪。

The bedposts **rattled**. The walls shook and in ones and twos, and then in dozens, the bugs started to fall to the floor with their legs in the air — **waving**.

Then the waving seemed slower.

啊！

噫！

床柱嘎嘎作響，牆壁搖晃振動，接著，一隻、二隻、數十隻電腦蟲紛紛跌落地板上，腳還朝著空中——抽搐著。

然後，電腦蟲的抽搐變慢了。

他們好像變小了！

他們確實在變小！

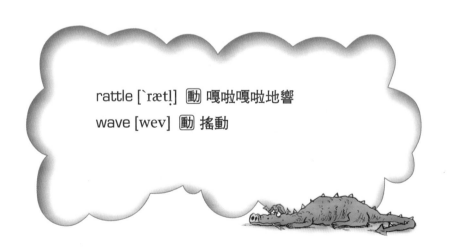

rattle [ˋrætl̩] 動 嘎啦嘎啦地響

wave [wev] 動 搖動

And so was Super Bug!

All of them **vanished**. (Well, all except
one in Georgie's bedroom.)

連蟲老大也變小了！

啊！

變小……

不！

變小……

……不見了！

所有的電腦蟲都不見了。（喔，還有一隻在喬琪的房間裡。）

vanish [ˋvænɪʃ] 勔 消失不見

The score was now:

Georgie & Cow 1,999,999	Bugs 1,999,994

Georgie could hardly **believe** it. Nor could the dragon. Hoarse **no longer**, he was talking to his children.

現在的比數為：

喬琪和牛　1,999,999

電腦蟲　1,999,994

呀呵！

我們成功了！

　　喬琪幾乎不敢相信，大龍也一樣不敢相信。他的聲音不再粗啞，正在對孩子們說話。

　　你們需要營養，孩子們！拿小女孩當晚餐如何？

　　嗯……我想我們該走了！

　　是啊……可是怎麼回去呢？

believe [bə`liv] 動 相信

no longer 不再

nourishment [`nɝɪʃmənt] 名 營養

damsel [`dæmzl] 名 少女

Chapter Nine

*W*hat happened next is a bit of a **mystery**. Mrs Bell was in a very bad mood.

Suddenly, seeing what she thought was a fly on the computer — it was the last bug — she **bashed** it...

...and **accidentally** pressed the EXIT key...

第九章

　　接下來發生的事情有點兒不可思議。貝兒太太很不高興。

　　哼！

　　她們一定在這兒！

　　突然，她看見電腦上有一隻蟲，她以為是蒼蠅——那是最後一隻電腦蟲——貝兒太太一巴掌打了下去……

　　啪！

　　……一不小心按到「跳出(EXIT)」鍵……

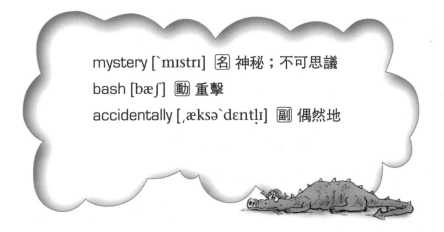

mystery [`mɪstrɪ] 名 神秘；不可思議

bash [bæʃ] 動 重擊

accidentally [,æksə`dɛntḷɪ] 副 偶然地

...sending Georgie and the Tank **hurtling** through time and space and the computer screen.

Seconds later, Mrs Bell found herself flat on her back.

……喬琪和唐可快速地穿過時空及電腦螢幕，她們被送回來了。

　　幾秒鐘後，貝兒太太發現自己躺在地板上。

　　嗨，媽！

　　你們看！

　　我想我們有訪客啦！

hurtle [`hɝtl] 動 飛馳

為孩子寫

~ 看的繪本＋聽的繪本　童話小天地最能捉住孩子的心 ~

嘘～趕快鑽進被窩，
爸爸媽媽甜蜜的說故事時間就要開始嘍

彩色的夢

🐟 **兒童文學叢書**

童話小天地

SAVOIR PLUS

專為十歲以上青少年設計的百科全書

人類文明小百科

行政院新聞局第十六次推介中小學生優良課外讀物

全套一共17冊／每冊定價250元

讓您的孩子發現文明，擁有世界

超級科學家系列
SUPER SCIENTISTS

中英對照，既可學英語又可了解偉人小故事哦！

當彗星掠過哈雷眼前，

當蘋果落在牛頓頭頂，

當電燈泡在愛迪生手中亮起……

一個個求知的心靈與真理所碰撞出的火花，

那就是《超級科學家系列》！

神祕元素：居禮夫人的故事　　含CD190元

望遠天際：伽利略的故事　　含CD190元

爆炸性的發現：諾貝爾的故事　　含CD190元

宇宙教授：愛因斯坦的故事　　含CD190元

電燈的發明：愛迪生的故事　　含CD190元

光的顏色：牛頓的故事　　定價160元

蠶寶寶的祕密：巴斯德的故事　　含CD190元

命運的彗星：哈雷的故事　　含CD190元

自然英語系列

你將會發現：學英語竟然可以這麼自自然然、輕輕鬆鬆！

自然英語會話

大西泰斗著／Paul C. McVay 著

用生動、簡單易懂的筆調，針對口語的特殊動詞表現、日常生活的口頭禪等方面，解說生活英語精髓，使你的英語會話更接近以英語為母語的人，更流利、更自然。

英文自然學習法（一）

大西泰斗著／Paul C. McVay 著

針對被動語態、時態、進行式與完成式、Wh-疑問句與關係詞等重點分析解說，讓你輕鬆掌握英文文法的竅門。

英文自然學習法（二）

大西泰斗著／Paul C. McVay 著

打破死背介系詞意義和片語的方式，將介系詞的各種衍生用法連繫起來，讓你自然掌握介系詞的感覺和精神。

英文自然學習法（三）

大西泰斗著／Paul C. McVay 著

運用「兔子和鴨子」的原理，解說PRESSURE的MUST、POWER的WILL、UP／DOWN／OUT／OFF等用法的基本感覺，以及所衍生出各式各樣精采豐富的意思，讓你簡單輕鬆活用英語！

國家圖書館出版品預行編目資料

喬琪與電腦蟲／Julia Jarman 著；Damon Burnard 繪；
刊欣媒體營造工作室譯――初版. ――臺北市：
三民，民
89面； 公分
中英對照
ISBN 957–14–3268–7（平裝）

1.英國語言一讀本

805.18　　　　　　　　　89010078

網際網路位址　http://www.sanmin.com.tw

ⓒ 喬琪與電腦蟲

著作人　Julia Jarman
繪圖者　Damon Burnard
譯　者　刊欣媒體營造工作室
發行人　劉振強
著作財
產權人　三民書局股份有限公司
　　　　臺北市復興北路三八六號
發行所　三民書局股份有限公司
　　　　地址／臺北市復興北路三八六號
　　　　電話／二五〇〇六六〇〇
　　　　郵撥／〇〇〇九九九八――五號
印刷所　三民書局股份有限公司
門市部　復北店／臺北市復興北路三八六號
　　　　重南店／臺北市重慶南路一段六十一號
初版一刷　中華民國八十九年十月
編　號　S85507
定　價　新臺幣貳佰伍拾元整
行政院新聞局登記證局版臺業字第〇二〇〇號

有著作權　不准侵害

ISBN　957–14–3268–7（平裝）

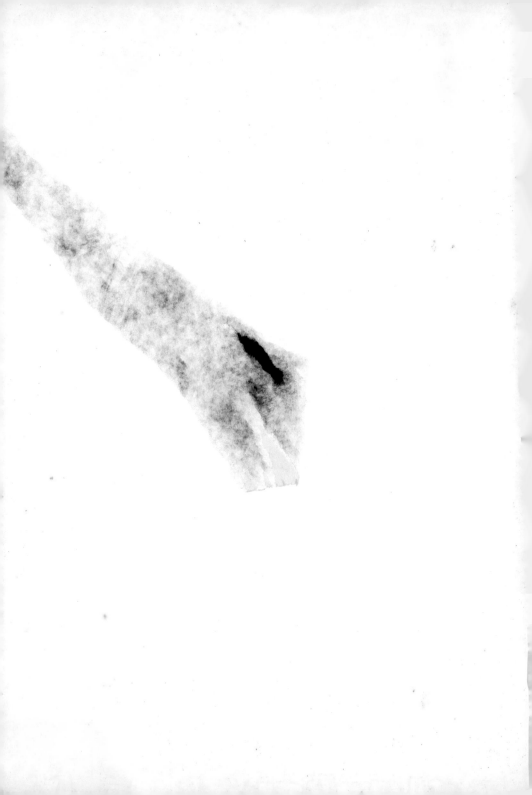